Peace of Mind

STOIC INSIGHTS

Carolyn J Sweers

Sweers
sweers@wi.rr.com
414 291 5981

Ordering Information:

For orders and inquiries, please contact:
1-888-375-9818
www.toplinkpublishing.com
bookorder@toplinkpublishing.com

Printed in the United States of America

CONTENTS

HOW TO READ THIS BOOK   1

WHAT IT MEANS TO BE A STOIC   5

THREE STOIC PHILOSOPHERS   9

THIRTY STOIC TOPICS   11

RECAP   65

HOW TO READ THIS BOOK

This is not a book that will explain something
and all you have to do is read it.
The Stoic insights are intended to
facilitate a direct encounter;
to start a "conversation":
a conversation with you, the reader, and your life
experiences.

"The unexamined life is no worth living." Socrates

No one needs to tell you
the best way to live.
You can find out for yourselves,
with the guidance of wise teachers,
which the Stoics are.

**In this little book,
you will be guided to reflect on your life
And to experiment with Stoic insights.**

**The best way to use this book
is to think of it as a kind of workbook.**

**Wide margins are provided for your notes and
reflections.**

**I recommend spending a few minutes each day on a
single topic.**
That kind of attentiveness will allow the passage to
speak
In ways that deepen understanding
and inspire beneficial actions.

There are thirty sections in this book;
thirty different but related topics.
You might want to consider doing one a day for a
month.
No need to do this in any particular order.
Be intuitive.
Use the topic list as a guide.

Experiment with pondering the selections randomly.
Different sequences will produce new insights.

From time to time, I offer specific reflection suggestions.
If these are helpful, use them.
If they are not, leave them alone.

If readers find this book helpful,
I would encourage them to
to read more widely in the Stoic literature.

A calm, receptive mind is important.
Each time,
before you begin,
spend a few minutes
sitting quietly
attentive to your breath.
This will help calm the mind
and make it receptive to what the words can teach.
Read the selection for the day.
Sit with it.
Let it evoke memories and insights as well as inspire
resolutions on how best to live the day.

Consider finding some like-minded people
to share the process with you.

The important thing is to
spend time with these words.

I cannot predict what time spent with the Stoics will do
for you.
I can predict
that whatever time you spend
is likely to be
beneficial.

WHAT IT MEANS TO BE A STOIC

A common view is that "Stoic" means impassive;
feeling no emotion.
"He was Stoic about it."
is a way to describe someone's reaction,
or lack of it,
to a great loss.

Stoics are calm.
But the calmness does not come from a denial of
emotions.
The calmness comes from an understanding of the link
between thoughts and emotions.

When we get upset,
it is because we have made the mental judgment
that what is happening is upsetting.
Someone else, in a similar situation,
might not get upset.
What causes the difference?

Answer: the INTERPRETATION of the situation.

If we change our judgments, our interpretations,
our feelings will respond.

How do we change our thoughts?
We change our thoughts
by learning to focus on how things are
rather than how we wish they were.

All things change,
sometimes rapidly.
If we fail to notice and/or refuse to accept this fact,
we are likely to get upset when circumstances change
and are less to our liking

Getting upset,
the Stoics say,
indicates a lack of perspective.
Not only do all things change,
they change in a vast universe
of which each individual human
Is a very tiny part

A good character cannot be harmed
no matter what happens.
In fact, a person who has made character
development a chief goal,
will have learned to use whatever happens
as a way to strengthen and improve character.
Stoic writers offer helpful advice.

The Stoic task is a demanding one.
You can't simply say, in a vague sort of way,
"Today I shall try to do better".
Not good enough.
Stoics are not talking about a self-improvement project
that you undertake for a week or two.
They are talking about **every** waking moment.
Do not let anything pull you away from what you need
to do.
Approach every action as if it were your last.
If you did that, the concentration would be intense.
Your mind would not wander.
You would not make excuses.

Try to avoid "discontent with your lot."
That will take practice.
But if you follow the Stoic suggestions,
you will gradually become
a master of yourself;
less prone to be led astray
by your own emotions
and by social pressures of various kinds.

**TRY IT
AND SEE!**

THREE STOIC PHILOSOPHERS

(and some suggestions for
how to take their advice.

Epictetus

Seneca

Marcus Aurelius

There are 30 topics in the pages that follow,
Each with quotations from Stoic writers.
I have tested these over and over again in my own
experience and invite readers to do the same.

STOIC TOPICS

Epictetus: 13
Causes of dissatisfaction
What is up to us and what is not
The importance of attitude
Avoid blame
Avoid wishful thinking
Why thoughts matter
How to train the mind
The importance of a cosmic perspective

Seneca: 29
What does a good life require?
Why life is long enough
Beware of expectations
Why complaining is a waste of time
How to cure envy
Why worry is a waste of time
Consolation in times of trouble
Don't trust circumstances

Marcus Aurelius: 43
Disquiet comes from within
How belief in Providence can be helpful
The importance of quiet times
Dealing with change
A warning about pleasure
Why pleasing people is not the point
Do not be seduced by fame
Be mindful of death
Take a healthy interest in other people

How to have a good character
Conform to Nature's ways
Never ask, "Why Me?"
What to do when upset
What to do when criticized

EPICTETUS

(55-136 CE)

For Epictetus, philosophy was a way of life.
He had once been a slave whose master permitted
him to attend the classes of a noted Stoic teacher.
When he was freed, he opened a school,
first in Rome, until the emperor banished philosophers,
then a new school in another location.
In his schools Epictetus taught people
how best to think about them selves
and to recognize the universe of which they are a part.
He instructed his pupils in the disciplines needed
to understand the nature of thoughts
as well as how to shape attitudes
in ways that reflect reality
rather than personal wishes.

Epictetus himself wrote nothing.
One of his students kept detailed and accurate notes
and it is from these
that we have access to Epictetus's teachings.
A major work is <u>Encheridion</u>
(sometimes translated as "Manual" or "Handbook").
The pages that follow contain insights from that work.

CAUSES OF DISSATISFACTION

What causes dissatisfaction?
A frequent cause is wishing life were different than it is.

Epictetus said:
it is not what happens that disturbs us
but our attitude about what happens.
Evidence for this is not hard to find.
Have you noticed how the same event
can produce quite different reactions?
For example, take the weather.
The person who had planned a picnic is upset because
it rains.
The farmer, on the other hand, whose crops
are badly in need of water,
greets the rain with relief.
Still others, whose life or work keeps them inside
may not be affected one way or the other.
The point is: no one has control over rain.
No one decides when it will happen or where or how
much.
Rain happens.
If we find the rain unsettling, we can change our
attitude
and in so doing
rid ourselves of frustration.
That may take practice!

**A major cause of inner distress
is wishing your life and its conditions were other than
they are.**
If you yourself can do something to make
improvements,
do it.
If there is nothing you can do,
you can still find peace
by accepting the conditions as they are
knowing that there is nothing so unfortunate
that a well- trained mind cannot find some value in it.
Remember:
the point is character development.
That is something over which we have control.

But what about negative times?
What is the best way to regard those?
Here, too, there are traps to avoid,
perhaps the greatest of which is self-pity.
"Why did this happen to ME?"
In a way, the Stoics say, the universe is doing you a
favor
by not treating you differently than any of its other
creations.
How it might disrupt the order of things if it made YOU
an exception.
If you can manage to keep in mind
that changes happen,
and some of them are not pleasant;
if you can learn to accept that that is simply the way
things are,
you can get keep perspective
no matter what happens.

WHAT IS UP TO US AND WHAT IS NOT

The key to peace of mind,
Epictetus said,
is to learn to distinguish between
what is up to us
and what is not
and to learn to accept what is not up to us.

Some things are in our power and some things are not.
If we confuse the two,
if we think something is up to us but it's really not,
we are likely to experience frustration and distress.

In some cases, it is easy to tell what is up to us and what
is not.
For example, the weather is not something that is up
to us.
Most of the events in the news are not up to us.
In fact, what people think of us is not really up to us,
either.

If we don't make the distinction, up to us and not up
to us,
and if we confuse the two by thinking something is up
to us
when it really isn't,
our lives will be much more frustrating and difficult.
Our minds will be agitated.
We will be unhappy.
We may take actions that make the situation worse.

A simple way to begin to recognize the difference
between what is up to us and what is not is to start is
with recent frustrations.
Begin small.
Start with relatively minor irritations
rather than major grievances.
(You can, with practice, work up to dealing with those.)

Make a list of what you have found frustrating or
irritating or annoying this past week.
Now for the hard part:
See if you can figure out
how much of what happened was outside your control.
Deal with specific cases one by one.

What did you learn by doing that?

THE IMPORTANCE OF ATTITUDE

**Epictetus said that what is up to us is our attitude;
our mental responses to situations.**
What disturbs us is not what happens
but our attitude about it.

It may be easier to see the truth of this
by considering the responses of other people.
For example, you go to a grocery store.
There are several people ahead of you in line.
The line does not seem to be moving
because there is an elderly person at the check-out
counter
who is slowly and carefully counting out coins to pay
his/her bill.
One person, obviously short on time, is venting
frustration:
"Why do they let people like that go to the store?
Why don't they open more check-out lines?"
Another person, a writer, is content to wait
because he/she enjoys observing other people
and getting ideas for writing projects.
Still another, who is empathetic to old people,
speaks calmly to the customer who is getting flustered.
A fourth person, who has picked up a magazine
with an article on the importance of noticing breath,
is taking advantage of the wait to practice what the
article suggests.

**Situations are as they are
but the responses to them are quite varied.**

If we can manage to keep in mind
that changes happen,
and some of them are not pleasant;
if we can learn to accept that that is simply the way
things are,
we will be able to maintain an inner equilibrium,
no matter what happens.

For peace of mind we have to recognize that our
attitude is always up to us.
For peace of mind,
We have to learn and practice
Taking control of our minds
and their reactions.

The process of learning to recognize what is up to us
and what is not,
is not easy
but worth it.
Any sort of success will bring with it
a sense of liberation.
Do some experiments.
See if this turns out to be true,
for YOU!

AVOID BLAME

**A common tendency is to think that the cause
of our feeling displeasure or anger or annoyance
is something or someone outside ourselves.**
"He (she) made me <u>so</u> angry!" is an expression often
said or heard.

The radicalness of the Stoic insight is
that it is not something or anything outside us that
causes the distress, it is our attitude toward it.

Yes, the loss is real.
Yes, the expected reaction was not given.
Yes, the present we sent was not acknowledged.
That is what happened.
The challenge is not to focus our attention outside
and engage in a blame game,
as if the discomfort we are feeling is someone else's
fault.
The challenge is to say to ourselves:
"O.K. This happened.
I don't like it.
In fact, I got upset.
But now what?
I can't change the fact that someone got what I
wanted.
It would have been nice if the person I just spoke
to had been nicer.
The gift I sent should have been acknowledged,
but it wasn't.

What are my choices
in the sorts of situations mentioned on the previous
page?

Make an issue about it and probably make the
situation worse? Complain to anyone who will listen to
try to get sympathy?
Continue to do what we think is right
no matter what reaction we get?

Remember,
say the Stoics,
it is difficulties that show us our true character.
What is important is not that the perceived misfortunes
happened.
Much about the situation was outside our power to
prevent.
What is important
is what character building choices
we make in response.

Take some examples from your recent life
and see what you discover when you take Epictetus's
advice.
Repeat frequently.
Take it as an ongoing challenge
to discover in any situation,
no matter how negative it may seem at first,
what value you can derive
that will help improve or strengthen your character.

AVOID WISHFUL THINKING

Try to avoid wishful thinking.
Try to avoid wishing what had happened had
happened differently
or
wishing that some desired event
would happen sometime soon.

Before you picked up this book,
what were you wishing you would like to have happen?
A change of circumstance?
More money?
A new love interest?
New and better friends?
More recognition?

Did you daydream about the changes you wished for?
Did you take any actions to make them a reality?

If you are honest,
does wishful thinking seem to be
a good use of your time?
why or why not?

Based on your past experiences of wanting things to be
different,
what did you learn that might be useful for you now?

If the change you hoped for happened,
was life better?
Or, did you keep wanting
something more?

WHY THOUGHTS MATTER

Without realizing it, we have developed mental habits
of which we may not be aware.
To become more aware,
Practice noticing your mental reactions.
At least once a day for a week or so,
make notes of your responses to situations:
both your judgments about the situation
(good, bad, liked, disliked)
and the emotions experienced
(anger, frustration, etc.)

What did you learn
By doing this exercise?

HOW TO TRAIN THE MIND

MEDITATION
The most important thing you can do
to learn about and train your mind
is to practice meditation.

There are many resources available to help with that.
Be intuitive.
Choose the method you think might work for you
and commit to a regular practice for a specified
amount of time.
Start with a week.
Then a month.

Taming the mind
is a challenging task
but well worth the effort.

Stick with a meditation practice,
even when you don't think it is working.

Some of the benefits of meditation will surface early
and will help you see the values of a regular practice.

The goal of learning to train the mind
Is not to suppress thoughts that seem negative.
Meditation is training in noticing;
not judging.

**The goal is to notice;
simply notice.**

Some thought patterns and reactions make our lives
more difficult.
They increase suffering and frustration.
Other thought patterns are more satisfying,
and more useful.

**From your own experience,
Try to find examples of both.**

Make a note of what these examples can teach you.

THE IMPORTANCE OF A COSMIC PERSPECTIVE

A cosmic perspective is central to the Stoic understanding
of human life and the best way to live.
There is a rational, providential order that governs all things.
It is important for humans to recognize this order
and their part in it.
It is important to align actions with
the order that nature provides.

What if one does not share this belief in a providential order?
Can this Stoic emphasis simply be ignored?
Not really.
The Stoics see no other path to peace of mind.

Try an experiment.
For a day or week or longer,
act **"as if"** there is some sort of cosmic scheme
of which you are a part.
Picture this any way you wish.

The important point is to regard one's life and one's actions
against as vast a backdrop as one can imagine.
As **Marcus Aurelius** put it:

**"This you must always bear in mind,
what is the nature of the whole,
and what is my nature,
and how this is related to that,
and what kind of a part it is of what kind of whole;
and there is no one who hinders you
from always doing and saying the things
that conform to the nature
of which you are a part."**
(II,9)

How short and fleeting is a human life.
And yet, in the relatively short time we have,
we can be AWARE of the Universe and its vastness;
we can see ourselves against the backdrop it provides
as well as recognize our kinship with it.

A cosmic perspective can open the mind
and with it the heart.
Try it and see.

SENECA

Seneca was born in Cordoba (Spain) sometime between 4 and 1 BCE and died in 65 of the Common Era. When he was a small child, an aunt took him to Rome where among other things he studied Stoic philosophy. He rose to a position of prominence in government and in the process acquired considerable wealth.

In the year 41, Seneca was accused of having an adulterous affair with the Emperor's sister. There is no clear evidence that this was so. Seneca's punishment was exile. One of his best known letters is the one he wrote to his mother to console her during his absence.

Seneca's exile ended when Nero's mother summoned him back to Rome to tutor her 12 year old son. When Nero became emperor, Seneca served as his official counselor and speech writer. However, over time, as Nero's mental health deteriorated, the relationship became so difficult that Seneca asked for and received permission to leave government service and lead a reclusive life. His changed circumstance, however, did not keep him from being accused, probably falsely, of participating in a plot to assassinate Nero. The Emperor ordered Seneca to commit suicide, which he did.

Note:
The quotes and paraphrases in the pages that follow
were taken from the book
Senaca: Dialogues and Letters
(translated by C.D.N. Costa, Penguin Classics)

WHAT DOES A GOOD LIFE REQUIRE?

Not a lot of stuff, Seneca said.
In fact, it is "nature's intention"
that there is no need for great equipment
to have a good life.
Anyone can do it;
though it does take work.

One has to realize what is important to do and be
and then live that way
and not just occasionally.

WHAT DO YOU THINK YOU CAN DO
TO HAVE A GOOD LIFE?

The good life,
Seneca said,
is a matter of character.
It involves choosing what is best,
no matter the circumstances.

External goods are nice.
Few would argue that.
But conditions change.

Fortunes are made;
Fortunes are lost.
But a good character,
once achieved,
Is not vulnerable to change or loss.

WHAT DO YOU THINK ABOUT THAT?

WHY LIFE IS LONG ENOUGH

It is not that we have a short time to live,
Seneca said,
but that we waste so much of it.

What are some of the ways we waste it?
How would you answer that question for yourself?

Stoics offer a list of ways people waste time
and put off or avoid developing a good character:
greedy desires,
giving into the seduction of wanting social approval,
grieving over things we can't change,
and being overly optimistic about what we can expect
from life.

People have a tendency to think that they are going to
live forever and this keeps them from paying attention
to important things
in the relatively short time they actually have.

Best to keep in mind that today may be your last,
and live accordingly.

IF YOU DID THAT,
WHAT MIGHT YOU DO DIFFERENTLY?

Match time's swiftness, Stoics say,
with speed in using it,

What might that advice mean to you
TODAY?

BEWARE OF EXPECTATIONS

Seneca said: "Beware of expectations."

Expectations might seem like a good thing
but **Seneca** warned against them.
Why?
Because expectations can be distractions
that take us away from the present moment and its
tasks.
As Seneca put it:
"You are arranging what lies in Fortune's control,
and abandoning what lies in yours."
("On the Shortness of Life")

Review some of your recent expectations.
What did reflecting on them teach you?

"We should... make ourselves flexible,
so that we do not pin our hopes too much
on our set plans."

Mental flexibility is an important skill to learn and
practice.
On that point, all Stoics agree.
There are so many changes that happen in life that
if we try to hold onto fixed views,
we are likely to be disturbed
when "reality" does not match our expectations.

With mental flexibility,
we can learn to adjust ourselves
to the possibilities and opportunities
offered by our specific circumstances.

No matter how uncomfortable
or disturbing
are life's changes,
we can use whatever happens
to make ourselves better.

**Think of some personal examples you can use
to experiment with this advice.**

WHY COMPLAINING IS A WASTE OF TIME

One of the pieces of advice Seneca gave to a person
who had asked how to achieve peace of mind was:
**"You have to get used to your circumstances,
complain about them as little as possible,
and grasp whatever advantage they have to offer.
No condition is so bitter
that a stable mind cannot find
some consolation in it."**

Why should we try to avoid complaining?

Examine your own experience of complaining.
What do you tend to complain about?
When?
Why?
How often?
What affect does your complaining have
on you
and on the situations?

The main problem with complaining
is that it puts the complainer at a moral disadvantage.

What does that mean?

Blaming puts the main problem outside,
with something we perceive to be negative
and which we did not choose.
Stoic advice?

What we can't change, we should accept.
What we can change,
our attitude and our character,
should be our focus.
So, complaining is a waste of time
that works against
the development of a character that is good.

What do you think about that?
Want to try some attitude experiments?

HOW TO CURE ENVY

**Focus not on what you lack
but what you have.**

Seneca had some practical advice for
those of us who think
life might be better
if we had what our friend or neighbor had.
Here is what he said:
**"Think of what you actually have:
possessions,
relationships,
personal qualities.
Think how poor your life would be without them.
Think about how badly you would want them
If you did not have them."**

Make a list of all the things you value in your present life
including your abilities and skills.
Make a list of specific relationships you have found
meaningful in your life, including now.
Make a list of possessions that you really like,
because they give you pleasure,
no matter what they cost.
Some will be gifts someone gave you.
Some will be items
You saved for and bought.
Others were chance finds
That caught your fancy.

After you have made the list,
Think how poor your life would be
if you did not have in it
the things you listed.

Could any **imagined** thing
bring you the satisfaction
that already lies within your own experience?

This reflection will help you recognize,
and appreciate,
the value of who you already are,
and what you already have.
The result?
Discontent with wanting something more or different
will diminish.
Try it and see.

WHY WORRY IS A WASTE OF TIME

If you are aware of a tendency to worry
and if, when you reflect,
you notice how unhelpful worry is,
the Stoics have some advice for you.

Anticipating difficulties,
worrying about them,
tends to be a waste of time.
As **Seneca** said in one of his letters,
"By worrying about the future.
we make ourselves miserable in the present."
And, if we are miserable in the present moment,
we are less likely to make good choices.

Seneca said:
"If you yourself can do something
to make improvements in your life,
do it.
If there is nothing you can do,
you can still find peace
by accepting the conditions as they are."

Remember: there is nothing so unfortunate
that a well- trained mind cannot find some value in it.
("On Tranquility of Mind")

**Review the actual circumstances of your present life,
including the persons or situations you find most
difficult.**
See if you can figure out what you could do
to use even the seemingly negative
material those provide
to improve your life.

For example,
Frustrating situations can be opportunities for practicing
patience.
Dealing with difficult people
can become opportunities for empathy
and compassion.

This is not an exercise to be done just once.
Put it on your schedule.
Do periodic reviews.
The more you train yourself to recognize
the character building potential in situations,
the easier it will become.
Try it and see.

**THE point is:
IMPROVE WHAT YOU CAN;
LEAVE THE REST ALONE.**

CONSOLATION IN TIMES OF TROUBLE

One of Seneca's claims to fame is the letters he wrote.
His model was "the Greek philosophical letter
written for instruction in how to live well."

One of the most remarkable letters Seneca ever wrote
was the one to his mother
to console her while he was in exile:
"Consolation to Helvia".

Seneca assured his mother that a good life
does not depend on material circumstances.
There is nothing about the exile experience, for example,
that can restrict his soul's growth,
unless he lets it.

Seneca also advised his mother to think of all the difficulties
she had already faced successfully
and to draw on those experiences for strength and
perspective.

He also advised her to drawn sustaining insights from
great literature and art.

As Seneca reminded his mother:
A good character is in no way dependent on externals;
it is not helped by favorable ones
nor harmed by those that seem negative.
Perhaps there is a letter
you could write to a friend who seems to be having
difficulties.
Based on what you are learning from the Stoics,
what could you say
that might be helpful?

DON'T TRUST CIRCUMSTANCES

Seneca knew from experience
how foolish it is to trust Fortune,
especially when times are good.
In fact, he said, those who are unprepared
for changes of fortune
tend to suffer more than those who are prepared.

**"Never have I trusted Fortune,
even when she seemed to offer peace.
All those blessings which she kindly bestowed on me—
money, public office, influence—
I relegated to a place whence she could
claim them back
without bothering me."**

**No person has been shattered by the blows of Fortune
unless he/she was first deceived by her favors."**

Fortune is not trustworthy.
It can give what seem to be blessings
and just as easily snatch them away.
If one trusted Fortune in good times,
one will feel betrayed
when misfortunes happen,
as they tend to do.

What is important,
no matter what happens,
is the character building choices we make in response.

Does misfortune make us more attuned
to the needs of others?
Do losses help us focus on the value of what remains?
Do difficulties activate positive new forms of coping?

If you review your own experiences with Stoic help
You are likely to discover that
no matter what happens,
no matter how great a misfortune it may seem to be,
you always have the power to put it to some use,
to improve your character.

**Isn't THAT
A liberating thought?**

Think of a personal example
you can use
to test this insight.

MARCUS AURELIUS

(121-180CE)

Marcus Aurelius was one of the Roman Emperors. Both of his parents died when he was quite young and he was raised by his grandfather. In his early 20's, he devoted himself to a study of Stoic philosophy; a study that would influence him for the rest of his life. He became Emperor in 161.

Aurelius began writing his <u>Meditations</u> in 170, presumably as a way to keep himself reminded of the Stoic principles by which he chose to live as he carried out the demanding duties of his office.

It is something of a minor miracle that the text survived but it has. It was first printed in 1559. George Long published an English translation of the Greek text in 1862. An updated edition of that text is available as an inexpensive Dover paperback. Most of the quotes are from that translation. A few, as noted, are from the Staniforth translation published by Penguin.

The <u>Meditations</u> are divided into "Books" and each book has numbered paragraphs. The numbers in parentheses provide the location.

I have chosen passages that have inspired and guided me over the years. I encourage all interested readers to get a copy of the <u>Meditations</u> and do their own exploring.

DISQUIET COMES FROM WITHIN

**"If you are pained by any external thing,
it is not this thing that disturbs you,
but your own judgment about it.
And it is in your power
to wipe out this judgment now."
(VIII,47)**

Disquiet can arise only from within.

The value something has for us
is the value our minds give it.
We have heard that over and over again.

If something external seems to be causing pain or distress,
Try to avoid a tendency to blame IT.
The problem is not what happened
but the **judgment** (interpretation)
that it is painful
or undeserved.

Try to see why what has happened is so distressing.
Did you have unrealistic expectations?
Did you think that you "deserved" better?

The Stoics insist that we have the power to make mental
changes.
That is something that is "up to us", as Epictetus would say.

To reduce mental stress,
Work on acquiring a "realistic" perspective.

**In what specific situations
Might this advice be helpful?**

HOW BELIEF IN PROVIDENCE CAN BE HELPFUL

**Belief in a divine providence that governs all things
is a core Stoic belief.**

As Marcus Aurelius put it in his <u>Meditations</u>:
**"Even that which is from chance
is not separated from nature
or without an interweaving and involution
with the things that are ordered by Providence." (II, 3)**

If you don't agree with that,
based on what you have experienced or heard,
try an experiment.
For a day or a week or longer,
assume the Stoics are right,
that there IS a divine providence that governs all things.

At the end of the time in which you tried the experiment,
ask yourself,
"Are there advantages to viewing life in this way?
If so, what?"
If you experience no advantages,
note that, too.

If you did experience some perspective benefits
by living "as if" the world is under the guidance of
divine providence,
consider finding ways to remember and practice this
awareness.

As for those of you who think you already believe
that the world is governed by divine providence,
see if your thoughts and actions bear this out.
Be as specific as you can.

THE IMPORTANCE OF QUIET TIMES

**"Do the external things that fall upon you
distract you?
Give yourself time to learn something new and good,
and cease to be whirled around." (II, 7)**

"Nowhere can a person find a quieter
or more untroubled retreat
than in his/her own soul,"
Aurelius said.

To act rightly, in the Stoic sense, the mind must be calm.
That is why it is important to find quiet places
both outside and within.
To go inward, even for a moment, is to temporarily
disconnect
from the pushes and pulls of external events.

**"People seek retreats for themselves,
houses in the country, seashores, and mountains;
[and you may have wished these, too.]
It is in your power whenever you choose
to retire into yourself.
For there is no retreat that is quieter or freer from trouble
IF you have cultivated a well-ordered mind."**
(Based on IV, 3)

Marcus Aurelius said that one of the best ways
to find peace of mind,
and to become free from the distractions that worries are,
is to "allow yourself a space of quiet".
It takes practice (and determination) to learn to be quiet.

Our minds have a tendency to be active,
flitting from topic to topic,
remembering,
planning,
prone to distractions.

Just as the surface of a lake is stirred up by wind,
so too is our mind stirred by various internal "winds".
When the inner winds die down,
gone are the restless thoughts.
What remains is an awareness that is calm and clear.

Whenever you feel disturbed, or worried,
or overwhelmed by things you think you have to do,
stop for a moment.
**Breath awareness
is a simple and reliable way to enter a quiet place.**

Sit quietly for a few minutes.
Focus attention on the breath.
Notice the in breath
and the out breath.
Notice what happens
in just a few minutes of doing this.

**Avail yourself often
of these times of renewal.**

DEALING WITH CHANGE

"How quickly all things disappear:
in the universe the bodies themselves,
but in time the memory of them." (II,12)

"Often think of the rapidity
with which things pass by and disappear.
For substance is like a river in a continual flow,
and the activities of things are in constant change,
and the causes work in infinite varieties;
and there is hardly anything
that stands still." (V, 23)

The rest of this page is left blank
so that you can make note of
the changes of which you are aware
and what your attitude should be about them.

Make some notes to yourself
about how you can benefit
by keeping life's changes in mind.

A WARNING ABOUT PLEASURE

How quickly all things disappear.
Remember that especially about the things
that attract you
with their promise of pleasure.

Can you think of some personal examples
that illustrate that point?

Don't avoid pleasure
But be aware of
the ways the allure of pleasure
can be deceptive.

NOTICING is important
as is self-control.

Self-control is a major Stoic emphasis.
Self-control is not a matter of forcefully imposing
restrictions on ourselves.
Rather, self-control is a matter of cultivating and fine-
tuning awareness
and becoming aware of the options we have
and to choose those actions that are truly beneficial to
ourselves
and to others.

Think of some specific situations you are facing.
What seems to be involved?
What choices do you have?
What choice would seem best
for all parties concerned?
Why?

WHY PLEASING OTHER PEOPLE IS NOT THE POINT

How important is it to try to please other people?
It is natural to want the approval of others.
A problem comes when the desire for that approval is
so strong
that one goes against one's own better judgment.
Marcus Aurelius's advice?
Make distinctions among opinions.
Consider the character of the people you try to please.
If you are honest, are these people admirable?
Can they help you to be your best self?
Do you find yourself going against your better
judgment
in trying to please them?
Are they using you and your regard for them
for their own self-centered purposes?
**What did you discover
when you asked yourself
these questions?**

The Stoics urge us
to learn to trust ourselves.
We should try to learn from the examples and opinions
of people
who can help with that,
and, if possible,
ignore the rest.

The only people's opinions
we should take seriously
are the opinions
that can help us
Improve.

**The opinions that should be taken seriously
are those of people we recognize as more advanced
in wisdom and goodness
than we are.**
These opinions can help us stay mindful
of what we really need to be and do.

**WHOSE OPINIONS SHOULD MATTER TO YOU AND WHY?
Be specific.**

DO NOT BE SEDUCED BY FAME

Even popular things
will not last very long
so don't pursue them unless they are good.
Use your head!
You will be beset by many opinions.
You may feel pressure to conform to what is current.
Don't be misled.

What popular people and things are most likely to attract YOU?
What can you learn by reflecting on that?

"Does the bubble reputation distract you?
Keep before your eyes the swift onset of oblivion,
and the abysses of eternity before us and behind;
mark how hollow are the echoes of applause,
how fickle and undiscerning the judgments of professed
admirers, and how puny the arena of human fame."
(IV, 3, Staniforth translation

To repeat:
no matter what the pressures,
never go against
your better judgment.

Think of specific situations where you could
apply that advice.

BE MINDFUL OF DEATH

The importance of death awareness:

**"Do not despise death,
but be well content with it,
since this, too,
is one of those things that nature wills."
(IX, 3)**

An awareness of **death** can have a disturbing effect.
The Stoics say it shouldn't.
The Stoics take a very matter of fact attitude
toward death.
We avoid thinking about it, they say,
because of the fears and fantasies we project
on what is in fact a natural process.

Things are born; things die.
There are no exceptions; not even us.

The remembrance of death can help us focus on what
is important.
It can diminish quarrels;
And make us more compassionate and generous.
Keep in mind the inevitability of death, the Stoics say.
If we recognize how short our time is
we may use that time
more wisely.

Be ever mindful
that you will one day die.
Do not let your imagination spook you
and make you turn away.
Death is simply a process of nature.
We can't change that fact
but we can use awareness of it
to more fully appreciate the present.

**Live every day AS IF it were your last
and try to get it right.**

If you want to experiment with this insight,
note the results in the space below.

HOW TO TAKE A HEALTHY INTEREST IN OTHER PEOPLE

What interest should we take in the lives of others?
Gossip is one of the pleasures many of us enjoy.
We like hearing the latest news about somebody we
know, especially if it has to do with some failure or
moral lapse.
The Stoics warn against this habit.
The problem with the kind of interest in others
that lends itself to gossip
is that it is a waste of time.
When our attention is focused on the faults of others,
we neglect our own.
Here is how Marcus Aurelius put it:
**"A good person does not look for faults in others
But stays mindful of ways he/she can improve."**

Review your own reactions to others.
Do you enjoy gossip?
Do you tend to look for faults in other people?
Do you try to find some good even in people you don't
like?

In several places Aurelius warned against
taking a curious interest in what our neighbor is doing.

**"Do not waste what remains of your life
in speculating about your neighbors,
unless with a view to some mutual benefit."**
(III,4, Staniforth translation)

Whatever interest we take in the lives of others
should have as its goal
a mutual benefit.

**If you took that advice today,
how would you live differently?**

HOW TO HAVE A GOOD CHARACTER

Marcus Aurelius made a list
of what a person of good character
should always keep in mind:

**Never value the advantages derived from
any of the following:**

Breaking promises.

Loss of self-respect.

Hatred and all forms of Ill-will.

Trying to damage or undermine the reputation of others.

Actions which you want to keep hidden.

Think of examples from your own life experience,
as well as observations of the behavior of others,
that support Aurelius's observations
that these sorts of behaviors
are not good.

CONFORM TO NATURE'S WAYS

"That which rules within,
when it is according to nature,
will always adapt itself easily
to that which is possible and is presented to it.
For it requires no definite material,
in moving toward its purpose.
(IV,1)

Think of specific examples from your own life
That can illustrate this point.

Remember:
The mind can circumvent all obstacles to action.
It can use whatever happens
To develop and strengthen a good character.

In every situation,
Ask yourself,
What is the MORAL response
That I should make?

Consider some specific situations in which you are
involved.
What would be different,
if you followed Aurelius's advice?

NEVER ASK: "WHY ME?"

Never say of any misfortune,
"Why ME?"
Recognize that what has happened
could happen to anybody.
Now that it has happened to you,
find ways in which the experience
can help you be better.
Nothing that happens
can keep you from doing that,
unless you let it.

Rather than saying,
"How unlucky I am that the trouble has happened,"
say rather,
how fortunate I am that it has not left me bitter
or anxious about the future.
Troubles happen to everyone
but not everyone knows how to stay calm."
When the mind is calm,
one can find opportunities
in what may, at first, seem like
a misfortune.

"'I am unhappy, because this has happened to me.'
Not so:
Say, "I am happy, though this has happened to me,
because I continue free from pain,
neither crushed by the present
nor fearing the future.'"
(IV, 49)

"Be like the promontory
against which the waves continually break;
but it stands firm
and tames the fury
of the water around it."

Can you do that?
Want to try?
What suggestions would you give yourself?

WHAT TO DO WHEN UPSET?

Marcus Aurelius has this advice:
**"If you are pained by any external thing,
it is not this thing that disturbs you,
but your own judgment about it.
And it is in your power to wipe out this judgment now.
But if anything in your own disposition gives you pain,
who hinders you from correcting your opinion?
And even if you are pained
because you are not doing some particular thing
that seems to you to be right,
why do you not rather act
than complain?"
(VIII, 47)**

**"When you have been compelled by circumstances
to be disturbed in a manner,
quickly return to yourself
and do not continue out of tune
longer than the compulsion lasts;
for you will have more mastery over the harmony
by continually recurring to it."
(VI, 11)**

Circumstances, at least some of them,
have a force that sometimes throws us off balance.

After being thrown off balance,
recover as quickly as possible.
This will take practice.

So, whenever you get upset,
try to recover your equanimity
as soon as you can.
That will help prevent you from doing things
you might later regret.

Just sitting quietly for a few moments,
focusing on the breath,
can bring about an instant and beneficial change.
"Habitual recurrence to the harmony will increase your
mastery of it",
said Aurelius,
speaking from experience.

Try it and see.

WHAT TO DO WHEN CRITICIZED

**"If anyone can show me,
and prove to me,
that I am wrong in thought or deed,
I will gladly change.
I seek the truth."
(6,21)**

This is a remarkable statement,
strikingly different from the way most of us deal with
criticism,
which is to get defensive.

Note carefully the phrase "if anyone can show me".
Ask for evidence.
Ask for proof, but in a non-defensive way.

Aurelius said that if such proof is offered,
he will "gladly" change.
Why?
Because self-improvement is his main goal
and anything that can help with that
is beneficial.

**It is only persistence in self-delusions and ignorance
which does real harm." (VI, 21)**

What to do about criticisms and suggestions for improvement? Some we should learn to ignore,
either because the person making them
has an incomplete understanding of the situation
or does not like us or what we are doing.
However, some suggestions for improvement
should be taken seriously,
because the one who makes them
is a good person
and has our best interests at heart.

So, when someone criticizes you,
And they can show you
That a change
Would be in your best interests,
Make the change.

That does not mean that we will like being corrected.
Even defensive reactions can provide valuable clues
about the changes we need to make
to improve our character.

Think of some specific examples
where you may have reacted negatively
to criticisms or suggestions for improvement.
Can you find any, that if you are honest,
you can now see would have helped you improve?
Be specific

RECAP

There are three major emphases in Stoic philosophy:

1. The importance of attitude.
2. The benefits of a cosmic perspective.
3. The importance of a commitment to creating
and maintaining
a good character.

These themes are interrelated.
For example, a good attitude,
which is essential for character development,
is helped by having a cosmic perspective;
a view of oneself
in relation to the universe.

TO BE A STOIC:

Work on attitude.
Cultivate a cosmic perspective.
Make a commitment
to creating and maintaining
a good character.

As Marcus Aurelius said:
"Every moment…do what you have in hand
with perfect and simple dignity
and feeling of affection and freedom and justice;
and…give yourself relief from all other thoughts.
And you will give yourself relief,
if you do every act of your life as if it were the last,
laying aside all carelessness,
passionate aversion from the commands of reason,
hypocrisy,
self-love,
and discontent with the portion that has been given
to you.
You see how few the things are, which
if possessed,
enable a person to live a life that flows in quiet." (II, 5)

Whatever happens,
we always have the power
to define for ourselves
the meaning of events
and to use whatever is provided
as a means to self-mastery
and moral improvement.

HOW TO HAVE PEACE OF MIND?

Do away with wishful thinking.
Cease to be at the mercy of strong wants and desires.
Limit time to the present.
Do not worry about the future
or about things you can't control.
Train the mind to be flexible and resilient.
Learn to recognize every experience for what it is.
Meditate upon your last hour.
Have a positive interest in the lives of others.

The Stoics provide insight.
What we have to do is PRACTICE!

CPSIA information can be obtained
at www.ICGtesting.com
Printed in the USA
FFHW021557131019
55527332-61335FF